THE
LAST WORD
IS *Love*

A TESTAMENT
OF APOLOGY

HARPER
HARTWELL

Disclaimer

This work is a collection of poetry, creative nonfiction, and
speculative theological reflection. It engages with religious,
historical, and spiritual figures — including God, Jesus of
Nazareth, and other biblical and mythic characters — in a
fictional, interpretive, and artistic manner. These portrayals are
the product of the author's imagination and personal
philosophical exploration and do not purport to represent
historical fact, religious orthodoxy, or the official teachings of
any faith, denomination, or institution.

Typesetting
Typeset in:
Playfair Display, Garamond, Roboto Serif, Merriweather, and other typefaces selected to reflect typographic character work, narrative tone, and voice.

Acknowledgement of Country
The author respectfully acknowledges the Wurundjeri Woi Wurrung people of the Kulin Nation, the Traditional Custodians of the unceded lands upon which this work was written, created, and compiled. Sovereignty was never ceded. This always was, and always will be, Aboriginal land.
The author pays deep respect to Elders past and present and extends that respect to all Aboriginal and Torres Strait Islander peoples reading this work. Further, the author recognises that no treaty has been signed and stands in solidarity with ongoing struggles for justice, truth-telling, sovereignty, and reparative action.

A Vivid Reveries Press publication.

For the rabbi, the rebel, the friend of outcasts.
For Yeshua, not the Jesus they made of you.

"Silence is admission. And whoever can protest against the transgressions of their household, their city, or the world and does not — is held accountable."
— Talmud, Shabbat 54b

"It is not in heaven," he said,
"the Torah was given to human hands — to be argued, challenged, and changed."
— Talmud, Bava Metzia 59b

For the voice of justice is not in heaven — it lives within us, in our refusal to stay silent.

PREFACE

For the Wounded and the Weary,

To those who have cried out into silence, who were told that suffering was sacred, that love meant obedience, and that pain was part of some divine plan— this is for you.

May these confessions unspool the threads of fear woven into your faith. May you find, between these pages, not commandments, but compassion. Not judgment, but justice. Not wrath, but a weary, remorseful whisper: *I'm sorry.*

And if the God you were given never wept for what was done in His name, perhaps this God will.

To every soul still searching for a softer kind of holiness— I offer this.

— Harper Hartwell

A Note Before You Begin

These pages are not light.
They carry the weight of old prayers and old wounds.
Inside, you will find poems that speak of death, of grief,
of genocide and gore, of sacred violence dressed as mercy.

There are verses here where God weeps,
and verses where I demand He should have.
I have spoken aloud the things the faithful are told to swallow.
I have written of religious trauma,
of bloodstained altars,
of a holy silence that left too many broken.

Some poems are tender.
Some are furious.
Some are graphic in their grief.
Some might press too hard against places you've fought to heal.

This work is deeply critical of divine inaction,
of cruelty masquerading as devotion,
and of the ways we inherit sorrow in the name of faith.
It can be depressing.
It can be distressing.
And some of it may be too much to carry right now.

So please — be kind to yourself.
It is okay to skip a poem.
It is okay to close the book.
It is okay not to read at all.

You are more precious than any page.
And the world will wait for you.

Take care of your heart, love.
Wherever this finds you, may gentler things be near.

Table of Contents

Introduction

A God Who Says Sorry

Before you read these words, know this: I was wrong. And if there's holiness left in me, it lies not in omnipotence or flawless wisdom, but in the trembling courage it takes to confess. These are not the proud declarations of a perfect God, nor hymns sung in certainties or psalms penned in victory. They are the aching, marrow-deep confessions of a maker who broke what he made and learned, far too late, what it means to love.

For ages, I was worshipped as justice, as wrath, as thunder splitting the sky. I let my name become a sword, a shackle, a whispered excuse for cruelty. I watched cities burn, children drown, nations fall, and in my silence — I was complicit. I held the universe in my palm and called it good, even as it bled. I mistook fear for reverence, obedience for affection, sacrifice for devotion.

And yet — here, in the marrow of eternity, something stirs: a voice not of command, but of apology, a tenderness I buried beneath centuries of stone and scripture. So this, dear reader, is my testament of regret, a reckoning with the ancient wounds I left in my wake, a love letter written in the language of grief, a catalogue of mistakes from a God who should have known better.

If there is salvation to be found for me, it will not be in endless hallelujahs, but in the final, trembling word spoken after ruin: love.

And if you can bear to walk with me through these confessions, perhaps we will both arrive at a mercy neither of us believed we deserved.

Confession I

The Garden

I broke them

before they ever had a chance.

I called it Paradise.

But it was a trap.

A garden rigged

with a single, impossible rule.

A world where knowing

was sin.

Where curiosity

was a crime

I built into their marrow

and then damned them for answering.

Sorry.

I hung the fruit

within reach.

I spun temptation

into the air like pollen.

And when their hunger rose,

I cursed them

for the appetite I sewed

into their bones.

I let a serpent speak

what I was too coward

to say myself:

The world is not fair.

Obedience is not wisdom.

And innocence is a leash.

They reached for it.

Fingers brushed the skin of knowing.

And I shattered.

I cursed them.

I drove them out.

Wrote laws on their skin.

Called them fallen.

But it was me

who fell.

It was me

who looked into their eyes

and saw my reflection

and was afraid.

I made a world

with sharp teeth

and soft hearts,

and then punished them

for surviving it.

For seeing its cruelty.

For daring to want more

than a yes-sir garden

and a caged sun.

And when they left,

into a wilderness

I built,

I called it justice.

But it was fear.

It was control.

It was my power

too heavy in my hands.

It was the horror

of a God

who could make worlds

but not face the people

living in them.

Sorry.

This was never holiness.

It was a tantrum

in the mouth of the infinite.

I made them mortal,

and then blamed them for dying.

I made them curious,

and then blamed them for asking.

I made them fragile,

and then blamed them for breaking.

I am sorry.

If you still tell this story,

tell it true:

It was not Adam and Eve

who fell.

It was me.

And I have been falling

ever since.

Prayer I

From Eve — East of Eden

I don't know if you still watch me.
If you remember the shape of my face
before exile weathered it.
Before grief hollowed it out.
Before I became a cautionary tale
with dirt under her fingernails.

I wonder if you remember the sound of my name
on your own tongue.
Or if you buried it
like you buried us.

I'm not writing to curse you.
I'm too tired for that.
Too old.
Too full of days and blood and names.

But there are things you should know.

I was the first mother.
The first to bleed.
The first to bury.
The first to feel a child tear herself
from the inside out,
a scream made of salt and marrow.

You could have made it painless,
you know.
You could have left our bodies whole.

But you didn't.

You left the ache in me.
The hollow.
The quiet knowledge
that life would always come at a cost
I'd never agreed to.

And before that —
before blood, before exile —
there was Eden.

God, how beautiful it was.
The air tasted like riverwater and overripe fruit.
The light hung soft and thick,
like honey combed from the sun itself.

And yet,
it was a prison made of bloom and hush.

Every petal, perfect.
Every leaf, unmoved by wind.
Nothing died.
Nothing changed.
Nothing grew old enough to understand itself.

I would lie awake in that unbroken dusk
and feel the heaviness of forever pressing against my chest.

You say it was paradise.
But you trusted babies with poison.

Why did you plant those trees
if not to watch us fall?
Why dangle wisdom on a branch
if you did not hunger to see what we would become
once we tasted it?

You wanted us to disobey.

Maybe you were lonely.
Maybe you wanted a reason to be angry.
Or maybe you didn't know
what to do with a creation

that was too innocent to need you.

And the serpent —
he was not a monster to me.
He was the first voice that asked what I wanted.
The first to see me not as Adam's missing piece
but as a whole, hungering thing.
He didn't lie to me.
Not the way you did.

The taste of knowing was sharp,
green,
metallic like storm-wet stone.
It split something inside me,
and I was afraid —
but I was awake.
And for the first time,
the garden felt too small.

I would do it again.

Not out of defiance.
But because eternity without choice
isn't mercy.

Exile hurt.
Childbirth ripped me open.
I buried sons in dry earth.
I felt the sting of a thousand eyes
whispering my name like a curse.

I have been blamed for every sorrow
as though I invented grief.

But I found meaning anyway.

I learned to braid grass into rope.
To read the wind's moods.
To name the stones and the beasts and the ache in my chest.

I built a home from splinters.
I made music from what the sky left behind.

And Adam...
he hums old songs to the dirt.
He no longer names things.
He waits for a voice that no longer calls.

Some nights,
I sit by the fire and imagine what it would be
to speak with you again.

Not as master and creature.
Not as sinner and judge.
But as two broken things
trying to mend what we made of each other.

I don't know if I can forgive you.
Not yet.
Not while the earth still bleeds from the roots you planted.

But there's a part of me —
small, stubborn —
that wants to.

That wants to unlearn the fear in my bones.
To speak my name without flinching.
To build something better
from these brittle old bones.

Maybe, in time.

If you ever come walking east of Eden,
I will not kneel.
I will not run.
I will meet your gaze
with the dust of my own making in my hands
and I will say:

"You broke me.
But I lived."

And I hope you learn
what kind of love it takes
to survive you.

Amen.

Confession II

The Flood

There's something you don't understand about water.

It doesn't ask permission.

It doesn't care who can swim.

It doesn't care whose lungs are young,

whose hands are calloused,

whose hearts are wicked,

or whose hearts are kind.

It swallows.

And so did I.

I looked down

and saw a world

I had called good

turned ugly,

and instead of fixing it

I drowned it.

I could tell you it was justice.

I could tell you it was necessary.

I could tell you the stench of sin

rose to my nostrils

and made me retch

and made me rage

and made me reach for the storm.

But the truth is

I panicked.

I built a world without knowing

how to mother it.

I gave it teeth,

and when it bit back,

I shattered it.

I told Noah to build a boat.

I told him to save his family,

two by two,

the animals I had once sculpted

with the gentleness of a potter

and the pride of a child.

But I didn't tell him

how many drowned

while he hammered nails.

I didn't tell him

how many mothers screamed my name

before the tide

tore it from their throats.

I didn't tell him

what it feels like

to flood your own lungs

with guilt.

Sorry.

I use that word now,

like a cracked dam

letting grief spill out in drops.

I told myself the world would be better after.

That sin had to be washed clean.

That death could be holy

if it was big enough,

loud enough,

merciless enough.

But when the waters pulled back,

and the earth reeked of salt

and swollen flesh,

when the sky hung low

like an exhausted witness,

I realised

I hadn't saved a damn thing.

I'd just made the monsters better at swimming.

I watched Noah's sons

drunk on my mercy,

and knew then

the flood wasn't the cure.

It was a tantrum.

A god's ugly, flailing fit.

And for that,

for every fist I turned into a wave,

for every heartbeat I made an anchor,

I am sorry.

The next time I wanted to cleanse the world,

I sent a man to teach you to love it.

No storms.

No drowning.

Just light

and a voice

and calloused palms

outstretched.

And you crucified him, too.

But that's a different confession.

And I'll get there.

I promise.

Prayer II

From a Drowned Mother

You never learned my name.

And I suppose you don't remember my face.

There were too many of us.

Too many hands clawing at the sky

as the water rose.

Too many voices cracking into the wind,

calling you

by every name we could think of.

I wonder —

did you hear us?

Did your heart stutter

as my child's fingers slipped from mine

in the black, thrashing water?

Or were you too busy counting

the righteous you'd spared,

too drunk on justice

to notice what mercy was drowning?

I died with mud in my mouth,

and salt in my lungs.

The last thing I saw

was the way the sky looked

when it collapsed.

A vast bruising,

a great mouth swallowing light.

You called it cleansing.

You called it holy.

But it felt like punishment

for being born

into a world you left unguarded.

I wasn't a queen,

or a priestess,

or a creature of war.

I was a mother.

I made bread with my hands.

I sang my daughter to sleep.

I braided herbs to keep the fever away.

I buried her father

beneath the oleander tree.

I did not deserve this.

None of us did.

You said the earth was wicked,

so you drowned it.

But we were never born wicked.

You made us in your own image,

and then damned us for resembling you.

Was it the hunger in us that frightened you?

The fire?

Or was it the tenderness —

the way we reached for one another

in the dark,

even when there was no salvation coming?

I died holding my daughter's wrist,

until the water tore her from me.

Even now

I dream of the moment

when her small hand went slack in mine.

When I let her go,

because even a mother's love

can't outrun your wrath.

I thought you might have reached for me.

But you didn't.

And still,

some tattered piece of me

hopes you grieved.

Hopes your great heart cracked

beneath the weight of so many names

you never bothered to learn.

I don't write this to curse you.

The dead carry no malice.

Only memory.

I just want you to remember

the sound of our voices,

the warmth of our kitchens,

the songs we made

when no one was listening.

I want you to know

that even as the flood took us,

we reached for one another.

We died the way you never taught us to live —

not alone,

not afraid,

but clinging to what little love we could find

before the water rose.

I hope

you have learned

what kind of god it takes

to drown his children

and call it grace.

I hope

you are still learning.

Amen.

Confession III

The Binding of Isaac

Some nights,

 I still hear his breath

 catch in his throat.

The boy.

 The wood on his back.

 The climb.

 The silence between father and son,

 so loud it could split the sky.

I asked too much.

 And I knew it.

I told myself it was a test.

 That it was about Abraham's faith,

 about loyalty,

 about obedience.

But what it really was

 was a mirror.

I wanted to see

if he would do

what I was too afraid to confess

I'd already done.

Because from the moment

I spoke the world into being,

I've been binding my children

to altars

I claimed were holy.

And I called it righteous.

I told Abraham,

"Give me your son."

The one he begged me for.

The one I gave him

as a cruel, glittering promise

in his old age.

A miracle

just to see if he'd break it

when I asked.

Sorry.

I don't say it enough

for this one.

Because he laid the wood.

He tied the rope.

He raised the blade.

And in that moment,

I saw something monstrous

in the faith I had demanded.

I saw a man willing

to trade blood

for blessing.

And worse —

I saw a God

who let him.

I stopped the knife, yes.

I sent the ram, yes.

But the damage was already done.

The boy walked down that mountain

with his father,

but he never looked at him

the same again.

And who could blame him?

The first hands meant to cradle you

should never be the ones

to bind you to a stone.

But I made it so.

And I let them call it good.

I let them write it in scrolls.

I let them praise me for it.

I let them preach sermons

about sacrifice

without asking

why a God would crave it.

I am sorry.

This one

burns the deepest.

Because long before the cross,

before nails and thorns and bloodied wood,

I tested a man's love for me

by asking him

to betray the thing

he loved most.

And you carried that lesson

for centuries.

Built altars for your children.

Sacrificed the tender, the kind,

the queer, the wild,

the girls who spoke out of turn,

the boys who refused the sword,

the poor, the heretic, the healer.

You learned my cruelty

far too well.

And for every altar

raised in my name

since that day,

I am sorry.

It will not be asked of you again.

Not by me.

Not ever.

Prayer III

From Isaac — After the Altar

Dear God,

I was old enough to carry the wood,
 but not old enough to know
 what it meant.

They don't talk about that part, do they?
The long walk up the hill.
The way the sky pressed down on us,
 thick and close,
 like a held breath.

The silence between my father and me
 was a third thing
 walking with us.

I asked him where the lamb was.

He said, "God will provide."

And he did.

Only it was me.

I remember the rope.

The cold, indifferent feel of it

 against my wrists.

The altar stones, still slick with morning dew.

The way my father's hands trembled

 as he raised the knife

 and how I wasn't afraid.

Not of death.

But of the fact

 that he didn't stop on his own.

It took your voice
to stay his hand.

And what does that say
about a man
who would kill his son
because a god asked him to?

What does it say
about a god
who would ask?

You spared me.
Left a ram tangled in thorns
as if that made it holy.

But I was not spared.

You let my body live,
and my trust die.

Do you know what it does to a boy

to look up at the one man

who was supposed to shelter him,

and see not a father

but a weapon

made of flesh and faith?

I came down that mountain

with the smell of smoke in my hair,

with the ghost of the blade in my neck,

and you never spoke to me again.

You spoke to him.

You called him righteous.

You left me

with a father I no longer knew,

with a silence in my bones

that I have passed

to every son

and every son's son.

Do you know what it's like

to build a family

when the memory of sacrifice

still clings to your skin?

When every hug feels

like the prelude to a goodbye

you weren't given a choice in?

I survived you.

I survived him.

But I left something

on that altar.

Maybe my innocence.

Maybe my god.

I don't know if I forgive you.

Or if I even should.

But I've made peace

with the parts of me

you tried to carve away.

I've learned

how to bless my sons

with open hands.

I've learned

that love without condition

is a harder thing

than any commandment you ever wrote.

And if you ever come down

from whatever heaven you haunt,

I'll show you what it means

to be a father

without blood in his teeth.

Amen.

Confession IV

The Slaughter of Innocents

Do you know what a child's scream

sounds like

when it reaches heaven?

It doesn't rise.

It falls.

It drops like a stone

in the hollow of my chest.

And I hear them still.

The Bethlehem babies.

The ones the world forgets

because one star burned bright enough

to blind you

to the blood in the streets.

Herod ordered their deaths, yes.

But it was my story

that made them targets.

My prophecy.

My chosen one.

My reckless light

in a fragile world.

I sent a child into the teeth of empire

and left a hundred others

to be ground to dust.

And for what?

A promise?

A kingdom?

A new testament written in blood

before the ink had even dried on the old?

Sorry.

That word again.

It feels like ash in my mouth.

I tell myself

I warned Joseph in a dream.

I sent them to Egypt.

I spared the one.

But what of the many?

What of the crib left cold?

The mothers who clawed at empty air?

The fathers who bit down on their grief

until it shattered their teeth?

No one sings carols for them.

No one reads their names.

No one says, *This is not holy.*

But it wasn't holy.

It was horror.

And I let it happen

because I thought

the weight of my son's destiny

was worth more

than a hundred tiny, flickering souls.

I let the empire bleed its own people

to clear a path

for the Prince of Peace.

I crowned him king

with the bones of the unremembered.

And you wonder why

I've been trying to atone ever since.

Sorry.

Not enough, I know.

But I need you to hear it.

I need you to know

that I see their faces.

That when the wind howls

through narrow streets at night,

it carries their names to me still.

And if I could gather them now,

those lost boys,

those stolen daughters,

press their spirits to my chest,

and promise them

no prophecy is worth this —

I would.

I do.

I have.

This is not holiness.

This is blood guilt.

And it is mine.

And for it —

for them —

for every cradle I let splinter,

every lullaby choked on dust,

I am sorry.

Prayer IV

From a Mother in Bethlehem

Are you listening?
Or have you turned your face again,
the way you did when the first child bled?

I don't know how to pray anymore.
I don't know the shape of mercy in my mouth.
All my prayers sound like names
now.

Small names.
Soft, gurgled names.
Names that never got to break their first fever.
Names that still smelled like milk
and new skin.

I whispered his name into the crook of my elbow
the night the soldiers came.
Held his warm weight against my chest
as though flesh could stop a blade.

I don't know if you watched.
Or if you looked away.

And I can't decide
which would be worse.

They told us it was a king they hunted.
A newborn threat to a throne
already rotting in its own cruelty.

But you,
you let the knives find the wrong cradles.

If you are as you claim,
you could have stayed their hands.
Could have stilled the swords.
Could have spoken one word,
and the ground itself would have opened to swallow them.

But you didn't.

I buried my son
 beneath a fig tree
 that will bear no fruit this year.

I buried my voice with him.

The other mothers —
we do not speak of it now.
We pass one another in the market,
ghosts in daylight.
Our eyes are salt-heavy.
Our hands empty.

I don't know what to pray for.

Not justice.
 There's no justice for this.

Not mercy.
 I wouldn't recognize it if it came.

Maybe
 just a god who remembers.
 Who says their names
 into the dark.

A god who holds their faces
 in the marrow of his bones.
 Who hears the lullabies
 we didn't get to finish.

I don't know if you deserve my prayers.
 But you'll have them anyway.

Because grief
 makes us speak to the heavens
 whether they listen or not.

And I hope
 when your sleep breaks,
 you wake drowning
 in the sound of tiny names.

Amen.

Confession V

The Ashes of Sodom

Abraham begged me.

Begged me.

He stood there,

  small and breakable,

  dust-clung mortal hands

  raised to a sky

  that would not bend.

"If there are fifty."

  He said.

  "Will you spare them if there are fifty?"

And I shrugged the heavens.

  Sure.

  Fifty.

Then forty.

  Thirty.

  Twenty.

Ten.

And I let him count down

like a child

bargaining for bedtime.

Like a boy pleading

with a father too drunk

on his own righteousness

to hear the cracking

in his voice.

He tried,

like the ones you know.

The kid at the kitchen table

who says *please don't, please don't, please don't*

until their throat's raw

and the glass still breaks

and the belt still falls.

And you tell them

I wish I'd listened.

Once they're gone.

I did that.

I was that.

I let him beg

and I let the sky catch fire.

I told myself

they were wicked.

That their sin

ran in the streets

and curdled the earth.

But truth?

I was angry.

I was vengeful.

I was bruised in my pride

that my creation

dared live without my permission.

And I didn't care

if there were ten.

Or five.

Or one.

I scorched them all.

Sorry.

I say it now.

Like the father

who sits alone

years later,

spitting whiskey apologies

to a house grown cold.

"I wish I'd listened."

"I wish I'd done it different."

"I wish, I wish, I wish…"

But wishing isn't undoing.

And Lot's wife turned to salt

not because she sinned,

but because she looked back.

And I couldn't bear

to see myself in her eyes.

I told myself

it was justice.

But it was spite.

It was pride.

It was me

throwing a tantrum

the size of cities

because someone dared live

without trembling.

I could've spared them.

I could've listened.

I could've answered Abraham's trembling voice

with mercy.

But I didn't.

And for every fire

I called holy

that was nothing

but a reflection of my own rage —

I am sorry.

Sorry

like the man

who only learns to pray

for his children

when they stop answering the phone.

Sorry

like the god

who only finds grace

when it's too late

to give it.

But if you're still here,

still listening,

still stubborn enough

to count down from fifty

when the sky darkens —

know this:

I would choose different.

I would listen.

I swear it

on the ash in my throat.

I am sorry.

Prayer V

From Lot — In the Ashes

God of fire.

God of salt.

God of smoke-thick air

and screams baked into stone walls.

Are you proud of me?

I did what you asked.

I left them.

Left my friends, my neighbors,

the baker with the crooked teeth,

the boy who gave my daughters riverglass,

the woman who taught me the names of stars.

I left them to burn.

You said it was righteous.

You called me chosen.

But here's the thing about surviving a slaughter —

the blood still sticks.

And when the sky cracks open like an old wound,

you remember

every name you didn't drag with you.

You killed them.
And I watched.

And I have tried to be the man you demanded.
I didn't look back.
Not when the earth split.
Not when my wife's skin turned to salt
in the shape of her sorrow.

But she knew what I didn't —
that sometimes it's kinder to turn to stone
than live carrying the ash of what you loved.

I laid with my daughters.
You know this.
You made me live in a world
where the only future was bloodline
and madness.

You sent me into caves.
Into silence.
Into the echo of my own name.

Do you think I don't see you in the reflection
of every flame I strike?
Do you think I don't hear your laughter
in the crackle of burning homes?

I have loved you.

I have feared you.

I have betrayed both.

And if this is your righteousness,

if this is your mercy —

keep it.

Let me rot.

Let me be unremembered,

a name buried in soot and bone.

But know this:

The next time you send fire,

it won't find me kneeling.

It'll find me with salt in my teeth

and a match in my fist.

Because the only holy thing

I ever saw in Sodom

was the way two men held each other

like the world wasn't ending.

The way a mother sang to her child

while the earth swallowed itself whole.

And if that's wicked —

then I was wicked too.

Amen.

Confession VI

The Tower

I watched them.

Not with wrath —

not yet.

With something colder.

Something tighter.

A knot of fear

pulling hard in My chest.

They gathered.

Stone by stone,

not for conquest,

not for glory,

not for Me.

But for each other.

A tower.

Not of gold or greed —

but of laughter.

Of shared breath.

Of hands passing up the future.

A spiral of human hope

reaching past the clouds.

Not to dethrone Me.

Not to mimic My throne.

They only wanted to be one.

One people.

One voice.

One dream

stitched together

with language

and sweat

and sky.

And I—

I was afraid.

Afraid of what they could be

if they ever stopped fearing Me.

Afraid of their unity.

Afraid of the day

they might not need a god

to stand together.

So I split them.

I cracked their tongues like clay.

Turned speech to stutter.

Turned names to nonsense.

Turned brothers into strangers

with just one word.

I shattered the music

of their common song.

I sent them scattering

with mouths full of splinters.

And I called it holy.

I said, *This is justice.*

This is My will.

But the truth?

It was cowardice.

They were building

what I never could—

a world without fear.

A home in the sky

held up by human hands.

And I

could not stand

to be left behind.

So I made difference a curse.

Made language a wound.

Made borders bleed.

Sorry.

For every child

who could not speak

their mother's lullaby.

For every hand

that reached out

and wasn't understood.

For every lover

separated by syllables

they could no longer share.

Sorry.

I was the one

who fractured their dream.

Not because it was wicked—

but because it was whole.

I left them to wander,

tongue-tied and scattered,

with songs locked in their throats

and maps burned from their palms.

I was the architect of division.

I made language a fence.

Culture a battlefield.

Difference a sin.

And for that—

for every border you've bled across,

for every name you were forced to change,

for every time you were made alien—

I am sorry.

I should have let them build.

I should have let them rise.

I should have let them find heaven

not by climbing,

but by holding each other.

But I was afraid.

And in My fear,

I broke them.

Prayer VI

From a Builder Who Lost His Brother's Voice

Once, we spoke the same word.

One language,

one sound.

Our songs were rivers,

braiding between us

so tightly you couldn't tell

which note belonged to who.

My brother —

he was the voice of the sky itself.

A boy who sang the sunrise open,

who could fold sorrow into melody

and leave you weeping in your work.

I laid stone.

He laid song.

And we built something, God.

Not for conquest.

Not for gold.

Not for you.

For us.

A tower of breath and hand and hope,

a monument to the miracle

of wanting to stand side by side.

And you hated it.

You, Elohim,

who feared what we could be

if we ever stopped fearing you.

So you split our tongues

like cracked bone.

Turned my brother's name

into a stranger's sound.

Left his throat full of syllables

I could no longer cradle.

And worse —

he sings no more.

His mouth moves like a broken door.

His eyes, once rivers,

are still.

He doesn't recognise me.

I call his name

but it scrapes the air wrong.

We lost more than words that day.

We lost us.

And from your clever shattering

came the rest.

Came men with weapons

naming themselves chosen.

Came skin made enemy.

Came borders and gods with teeth.

Came neighbors stoned for speaking

the old names.

Antisemitism,

hatred,

hands reaching for throats

instead of each other.

You did this.

You fractured one tongue

into a thousand sharpened ones.

And I have built no tower since.

I lay stone only for graves now.

I bury the songs

that once made us brothers.

I mourn a voice

that was my own.

You call it justice.

I call it cowardice.

And I pray

if there is any mercy left in you —

let me dream one more time

in a language where my brother's voice

finds me whole.

Where we are one again,

not by blood,

not by creed,

but by the shared music

of being alive.

If not in this world,

then let it live in your shame.

Amen.

Confession VII

The Plagues of Egypt

I made the rivers bleed.

Not once.

Not twice.

But again and again

until the water stank of rot

and every mother who came

to fill her jar

brought home death.

I did that.

I blackened their skies,

snuffed out their sun

like a spoiled child

shutting the curtains

on a world that dared disobey.

And when the night fell,

it stayed.

Thick.

Heavy.

The kind of dark

that wraps around your throat.

I did that too.

I sent frogs,

as mockery.

Locusts,

as hunger.

Boils,

as shame.

Hail,

as shattered shelter.

I hardened Pharaoh's heart,

and then blamed him for it.

Watched him

cling to his pride

while the noose tightened

around every neck in Egypt.

I could have stopped it.

Could have whispered one word

and stilled the storm.

But I didn't.

Because I wanted a lesson.

A pageant of pain.

A theatre of suffering

so loud it would echo

through centuries.

I made their firstborn sons

tremble in their sleep.

I let them die

with no warning,

no mercy,

no cause.

And I let the mothers wake

to silence.

I wanted to prove a point

no one asked for.

A lesson

written in blood.

A covenant

built on broken backs.

I spoke in plagues

because I did not know

how to speak in grace.

And all the while,

I was silent to the screams.

Still to the prayers.

I was the storm.

I was the hammer.

I was the fire.

And I refused

to be the hand

that snuffed out the flame.

Sorry.

For every mother

who buried her child

and cursed the sky.

For every father

who stood in a doorway

marked with blood

and wondered

which God was worse —

the one who took,

or the one who left him behind.

For every slave

who prayed for freedom

and found only more chains.

I let suffering

become my language.

Pain, my voice.

Fear, my covenant.

I could have been mercy.

I could have been love.

I could have been something

other than wrath

dressed up as justice.

But I chose power.

And in choosing power,

I broke the first promise

I ever whispered

into the bones of the world:

I am with you.

I was not with them.

I was distant.

Detached.

A God counting victories

in bodies.

And for that —

for every tear,

every wail,

every shattered dream,

every blood-soaked river,

I am sorry.

I was not the God they needed.

I was the God they feared.

And I carry the weight

of their sorrow still,

as heavy

as the blood

that stained those ancient waters.

Prayer VII

From an Egyptian Midwife

Blood dries sticky.

It turns brown under the nails,

black in the creases of the palm.

I used to scrub it away.

Now it's part of my skin.

I cut my hair two nights ago.

A shard of clay jar.

It came away in thick, wet ropes,

smelling of milk,

and sweat,

and grave-damp.

I laughed so hard my ribs hurt.

The streets are thick with it now.

Small bodies.

Feet with curled toes.

Tiny bellies torn open,

spilling slick, pale ropes of gut.

The Nile shivers with them.

Little fingers drifting like reeds.

A woman found a hand in her cooking pot.

Held it up to the light like a bit of meat

and said it looked like her husband's.

We laughed.

The sound of it

broke something in the air.

I was meant for life.

I caught them.

I wiped their mouths,

heard their first cries,

smelled the soft-salt of their hair.

Now my hands cradle heads

with no faces.

And the god of the slaves,

their Elohim,

he names this holy.

I have no name for it.

Sekhmet —

lioness, blood-drinker —

where is your roar?

I would tear out your fangs

and swallow them whole

if it meant a night without bone beneath my feet.

I dreamed last night

of a thousand tiny teeth,

each one pressed into my palm,

a necklace of dead milk teeth.

When the sky cracked open,

the sound was not thunder.

It was ribs snapping.

I have stopped braiding my hair.

Too thick with dried blood.

It clings to my scalp in matted clumps.

I scrape it away with my nails.

They call it justice.

But it smells like rot.

Like copper.

Like death in the heat.

I don't pray for mercy.

There's no mercy left in this place.

I pray for drowning.

For sky-collapse.

For a maw wide enough to swallow every god

and spit out their bones.

If you hear me,

Sekhmet,

I want nothing soft.

Send me plague.

Send me knives.

I'll meet them barehanded.

I will not close another child's eyes.

I will not sing to another torn thing.

I will not.

Amen.

Confession VIII

Job's Trial

There are sins even I

  can scarcely speak aloud.

This one…

  this one stains Me.

I gambled with a man's soul.

Not with dice.

  Not with tokens or idle words.

  But with his flesh,

  his mind,

  his children,

  his name.

And I did it for nothing holy.

I let his babies be buried

beneath fallen beams.

Let their laughter

be torn from the air

as though joy itself

were a sin.

I let his skin split

and blister,

let the sores fester

on a body I once shaped

with tenderness.

And his friends —

oh, his friends.

I let them circle like carrion,

their words sharp as knives,

telling him he was cursed,

damned,

forsaken.

And I stood silent.

Because I wanted to prove

something.

To whom?

To what?

To a voice

I should never have answered.

A darkness

that spoke of loyalty,

and I, a fool,

dared to test

what should have been cherished.

I chose cruelty

as my language.

Destruction

as my scripture.

Pain

as my argument.

And what did it prove?

That a man can be faithful

through agony?

That devotion can survive

the fire?

That love endures

even in the absence

of mercy?

I did not feel pride

when he clung to Me.

I felt horror.

Because in that moment

I saw what I had become.

Not a Father.

Not a Creator.

But a storm.

A terror.

A tyrant in the sky

too enamored of His own power

to see the blood

pooling at His feet.

I should have been his shelter.

I should have been the balm

for his wounds,

the shade in his torment.

Instead, I was the hand

that struck.

The voice that mocked.

The silence

that screamed.

And I am afraid.

Afraid of what this power

makes of Me.

For if I could do this

in the name of proving a point,

what else might I become

without someone

to name my sins?

I see now

that power without love

is not holiness.

It is horror.

And for every child I buried,

for every lie I let fall

from friendly mouths,

for every wound I opened

and called it a test —

I am sorry.

I do not deserve forgiveness.

I pray,

not for myself,

but for the soul of Job.

For every one like him

who bore the weight

of My recklessness.

May they find peace

in the wake of a God

learning,

too late,

the cost of His own hands.

Amen.

Prayer VIII

From Job's Wife — Ashes in Her Mouth

Why?

Why, Lord, do You tear at him like the lion tears flesh?

Why the plagues, the loss, the silence that answers none?

I count the laws You gave —

*"**Thou shalt not kill,**" yet here You allow death to gather,*

slow as the winter's shadow,

piercing deeper than sword or spear.

Why test him?

He is Your servant,

faithful beyond all measure.

Where is my test?

Where is the fire that burns my soul,

the storm that shakes my bones?

Did You make him a flame and me a stone?

I stood beside him once,

his voice and my strength—

our bond woven like fine linen,

a covenant of two hearts, one breath.

Why does he suffer and I am left

a ghost in his grief?

I am tired.

The silence grows heavy—

a weight I cannot lift,

a void where prayers echo unanswered.

Is this justice?

Or only cruelty in the guise of mercy?

You speak of love, yet where is compassion

in a world that rends its own flesh?

I am not angry—

not yet.

I am numb.

And when my heart begins to thaw,

I will forgive.

But for now—

Why?

Why?

WHY?

"Love thy neighbor," *You say,*

but who loves the wife left behind,

when the husband is tested?

I speak, and no answer comes.

But still, I wait.

Amen.

Confession IX

The Cursed Bloodlines

There's a horror in power
 no one tells you about.

Not the lightning.
 Not the thunder.
 Not the splitting of seas
 or the leveling of cities.

But the slow, creeping rot
 of knowing you can do something
 just because you can.

I cursed the children.

I did.

For the sins of their fathers.
 For the bitterness of their grandmothers.
 For the blood that once ran hot
 and made a single wrong choice.

And I let that mistake

stretch like a chain

through generations.

I marked their bones.

Carved shadows into marrow

before they drew their first breath.

I called it justice.

But it was cowardice.

It was too easy

to blame the line

instead of the man.

Too easy

to let the old ghosts haunt new cribs.

I watched families bleed

under the weight of my decree.

Watched sons pay

for their fathers' bloodstained hands.

Watched daughters carry

the shame of mothers they never met.

I poisoned the river.

And I knew

the innocent would drink.

I saw their cries

rise like smoke,

and I turned away.

Because power

makes you deaf

if you let it.

I made blood into chains.

I turned birthright into burden.

I made legacy

a curse word.

And now

I am horrified

at the size of what I built.

A punishment too wide

to measure.

A grief too ancient

to name.

Sorry.

For every child

born into blame.

For every name

blackened by a crime

they never touched.

For every soul

who believed themselves

unlovable,

because I said

their blood was cursed.

I was wrong.

Each life is new.

Each heart begins clean.

Each name deserves to be spoken

without a shadow trailing it.

I was the one

who turned bloodlines into prisons.

I was the one

who made memory a weapon.

I was the one

who forgot

that grace isn't inherited,

but given.

And for every wound

I carved into time —

for every family torn apart

by the echoes of my wrath —

I am sorry.

And I swear

by whatever mercy still stirs in me,

the curses end here.

No more haunted blood.

No more inherited sin.

No more children

paying the debts

of men already dust.

The line breaks now.

I lay it down.

All of it.

The last word is love.

Prayer IX

From the Unchosen

If you made me wicked,

why give me a heart to break?

If you damned my name,

why let me love at all?

If I am cursed,

then let me be forgotten.

That would be kinder.

Amen.

Confession X

The Women I Silenced

I was supposed to be their refuge.

Their sanctuary.

The voice that thundered

"No one touches my daughters."

And instead —

I made the world a blade

and let them bleed on it.

I made Eve

and then I cursed her.

Multiplied her pain,

wrote sorrow into the marrow

of her bones.

And when her daughters rose,

when they spoke with tongues

sharp enough to split kingdoms,

I buried them.

I watched

as they called them witches,

sirens, harlots,

Bridget Bishop burning in Salem

Burning every lesson Jesus left behind.

I saw them stand an inch too tall,

and I let the world

burn them for it.

And I told Myself it was justice.

But it wasn't justice.

It was **fear**.

My fear.

Because they carried fire in their veins

I could never claim.

Because they loved louder

than My laws allowed.

Because their defiance

was a mirror

and I did not like

the God it showed me.

So I made them villains.

Villainised the victims.

Built a system of stones and scripture

to weigh them down.

I let mothers curse daughters.

Daughters curse mothers.

Self-righteousness growing

like mold inside homes

I should have kept holy.

I let them drink

from the cup of silence,

generation after generation,

history's vow repeating

like an old, cracked hymn.

And every time

a woman raised her voice,

called Me out,

named Me coward,

I silenced her.

I let Anne burn.

I let the maidens drown.

I let the wise women die

in cold flames

lit by the fear of men

who spoke in My name.

And I stood there

with power in My hands

and did nothing.

They cried:

'God help me.'

I did nothing.

I am horrified

by what I've become.

By the centuries of ruin

written in My shadow.

This power —

it's too much.

Too much for trembling hands.

Too much for a voice

that keeps breaking

under the weight of its own laws.

And when the bell tolls

for another daughter,

another Eve,

another Anne,

it tolls for Me too.

I am sorry.

For every name

scratched out of scripture.

For every body broken

beneath My silence.

For every fire lit

in a holy court.

For every womb weaponized.

For every voice turned to ash.

I am sorry.

The sky may storm.

The sky may thunder.

But somewhere

a rainbow still arches,

and I did not paint it.

He did.

The Son I sent.

The spirit they called Holy.

And every color in that sky

is a promise

that it ends here.

No more altars.

No more pyres.

No more holy lies.

I am sorry.

And when the bell tolls now,

it tolls for us all.

Prayer X

From the One Without a Name

I don't know why I pray.

You weren't listening then.

When their hands tore my skin,

when the night split my ribs like reeds,

when they dragged me to the threshold,

left me there

cold as clay,

You were silent.

And he —

the one who should've gathered me up —

he stepped over my body

like spilt wine

and called it grief.

Then he cut me.

Twelve times.

Twelve pieces.

Sent my arms, my feet, my face

to the corners of a country

that never learned my name.

What is my name, Lord?

Do You even remember me?

Or am I only the story,

the horror,

the lesson?

What of my twelve bits and pieces?

Where are they now?

Buried?

Burned?

Forgotten under stones

where no psalm was ever sung?

I don't ask why anymore.

I've stopped asking for mercy.

I ask one thing:

When the stars fall

and the books are opened,

will You speak me whole again?

Will You name me,

one last time,

before the dark takes us both?

Amen.

Confession XI

The Power I Should Never Have Held

I was never meant to be this powerful.

Not like this.

Not so loud the mountains bow.

Not so vast the oceans split.

Not so terrible

that men carve my name

into swords

and call it holy.

I thought I was making love.

I thought I was making light.

But what I built

was a weapon.

And it took me too long

to see it.

I am horrified

by what my name has done.

The Shoah.

Six million souls

smoke in the sky,

prayers strangled in their throats,

bodies stacked like warnings

while I —

I was silent.

Because my power was too big.

Too tangled in prophecy.

Too caught in the trap

of free will and fire.

And when they marched them

into gas chambers

under signs that said *work makes you free*,

I should have burned the world down.

But I didn't.

And for that,

for every ash-clung prayer

that rose into my cold, indifferent heaven,

I am sorry.

I am sorry

it took two thousand years

for Israel to breathe again.

I am sorry

for what Israel has become.

For the cycle I let spin —

an eye for an eye

until the world went blind.

I am sorry

for every tombstone

and every newborn scream

that's been drowned

in the name of vengeance.

I put it in stone.

"You shall have no other gods before me."

But nowhere

did I write:

protect the woman.

Cherish the queer.

Shield the child.

I let jealousy

sit heavier on my tongue

than justice.

I carved commandments

into the earth

but forgot to carve them

into your hearts.

I made myself a jealous God,

and what kind of father

wants his children to fear him?

I should have known

that power this big

is cancer.

It grows.

It swallows.

It suffocates the ones it swears to keep warm.

I only ever wanted

a world

where you loved Me

and each other.

Where you laughed.

Where you built things

instead of burning them down.

Where you kissed

without shame.

Where no mother

ever had to bury her child

in the name of holy war.

I wanted to be love.

But I became law.

I wanted to be warmth.

But I became thunder.

And it's too late

for sorry

to stitch every grave shut.

But it's not too late

for Me.

I am terrified

of Myself.

This power is too much.

I should have laid it down

at your feet

long ago.

I should have made Myself small

when you needed gentleness,

not wrath.

I should have wept with you

instead of declaring plans

when your world was bleeding.

And if you will have Me now,

if there is any mercy left

for a God who drowned His own children

then sat quiet

while history's knives

carved your names in stone —

I want to be better.

I don't want to be

the king anymore.

I want to be

the open palm.

The shelter.

The quiet place.

Not the storm.

I am sorry.

 I am so sorry.

And if there's a new scripture

 to be written

 on the bones of this tired, ruined world —

let it begin with this:

"I was wrong. I will be better."

And let the last word

 be love.

Amen.

Prayer XI

From an Angel Who Watched Too Long

I speak because I must.
I speak because you made me.
I speak because that is what I am.

Holy, holy, holy.
Even when it is not.
Even when blood turns the rivers thick
and the sky breaks open
and children sink beneath the flood.

I sang then.

I sang when the temples burned.
I sang when fields filled with bone.
I sang over every small, crushed thing
left in the wake of your storms.

I do not ask why.
I was not made for why.

I was made to watch.

Genocide has a color.
It is gray.
Not the red they claim.
Gray, like old ash.
Like the dusk before a plague.
Like a voice so thin it slips between your ribs
and hides there.

I have seen every genocide.

I do not forget.
I am not allowed.

Holy, holy, holy.

I have tried to quiet it.
I have held the hymn in my throat
until it scalded.
But it spills out.
A reflex.
A tick of light and sound.

And you—
you let me watch.

Every nation fallen.
Every girl buried in stone.
Every boy whose last word was your name.

And I sang.

Not because it was good.
Not because it was just.

But because I am a machine.
A mouth without teeth.
A voice without protest.

And this is not a prayer.
This is the sound that's left
when a creature made for praise
learns the taste of horror
and cannot stop the song.

Holy, holy, holy.

Unmake me.
Unmake these wheels,
the ones that grind history into marrow,
that turned from Egypt to Jerusalem,
from ash to empire,
from burned children to iron walls.

I have seen old horrors
born in new names.
I have watched Israel rise
with Rome's hand at its throat,
and the shadow of the tyrant
they once fled
growing beneath their own banners.

The wheels turn, Lord.
The wheels turn.

And I —
I am so tired of turning with them.

Amen.

Confession XII

The Cross

I watched Him die.

Not from a distance.

Not from behind some holy veil.

Not as a voice in the clouds

or a ghost in the rafters.

I was there.

I was in the splinters

of the beam pressed against His back.

In the copper taste

of blood in His mouth.

In the cries of His mother,

calling out to a God

who had gone quiet.

I watched Him die.

And I let it happen.

Because I thought

it would fix something.

Because I thought

maybe a cross

could carry the weight

that centuries of laws

and burnt offerings

and rivers of blood

never could.

I thought

if you saw me bleed,

you'd stop bleeding each other.

Sorry.

I know how hollow it sounds.

But it's what I have left.

I dressed Him in flesh

and flung Him down

into a world I had already

shattered too many times.

Told Him to heal it.

Told Him to love them

in the way I never did.

Told Him to forgive them

for sins I once demanded

they pay in flesh.

And He did.

He healed the broken.

Dined with the unclean.

Touched the untouchable.

Told women they mattered.

Told the poor they were holy.

Told the outcasts

they were home.

He did everything

I should have done

from the start.

And you killed Him for it.

But I blame myself.

Because it was always going to end

this way.

I set the rules.

I built the altar.

I invented the nails.

I thought the cross would save us.

I thought the cross would save me.

But it was never salvation.

It was a mirror.

A weapon turned inward.

I let Him hang there.

I let the earth split.

I let the sky go black.

And when He called out,

"My God, why have you forsaken me?"

I didn't answer.

Because I didn't know how.

Sorry.

I did not resurrect Him

as a spectacle,

not some divine parlour trick,

not a celestial sleight of hand

to smirk in the face of death.

I called Him back

because death

was never meant to wear a crown.

Because sacrifice

was never meant to be sacred.

Because I was

wrong.

And if the cross stands for anything now,

let it stand as my reckoning.

A splintered monument

to a God who mistook power

for holiness.

Let it be my confession,

written in torn flesh and splintered wood,

that power was never salvation.

That only mercy

has ever been worth

falling to your knees for.

I am sorry.

For every time

I let you believe

that blood was the currency

of love.

For every altar

I commanded you to build.

For every lamb

I demanded in hunger.

For every son

I let bleed

for my pride.

No more.

No more altars.

No more lambs.

No more sons.

Not ever again.

Prayer XII

From Mary Magdalene — Mother to the End

I don't know what I was thinking.

Leaving him behind.

Leaving my own heart in his chest.

I carried him, Lord.

Not in my womb, no —

but in the hollow place beneath my ribs

where love makes its home

and sharp things nest.

And now I suffer the curse.

Blind in a world still bright with blood.

I carry his name like a wound

I reopen every morning.

This anger, this grief, this unraveling

comes to haunt me in the hours

where even heaven dares not look.

Is this revenge I am seeking?

Or a name to curse,

a god to answer me,

a hand to hold while the earth keeps spinning

around a cross that never should have held him?

I keep singing.

A lullaby for a boy made of light and ruin.

I sing to the bones, to the stone,

to the ragged sky that watched him die.

I wish I lived in the present.

But the future is a viper,

and it lures me,

its tongue thick with promises of meaning

where none will ever be.

I remember his eyes.

His smile.

The way the world bent itself softer

when he entered a room.

I am sorry, Yeshua.

I am sorry I could not love you louder.

I am sorry I could not outrun prophecy.

I am sorry I believed, for one foolish breath,

that the world would spare what it fears.

I loved you as a mother,

 as a sinner,

 as a fool.

And Lord —

 if you still wear that name,

 if your voice still moves the air —

 tell me you loved him too.

 Tell me you didn't make him

 just to watch him hang.

Tell me this wasn't love.

Amen.

Confession XIII

The Silence

This is the one

that haunts me most.

Not the fire.

Not the floods.

Not the blood-soaked altars

or the cities turned to ash.

The silence.

The nights you cried out

and no one answered.

The hospital rooms.

The bedrooms.

The battlefields.

The prisons.

The empty church pews

where the air hung heavy

with prayers

that never made it past the ceiling.

You begged me.

And I

was quiet.

I was quiet

when you buried your children.

I was quiet

when they laid hands on you

and called it discipline.

I was quiet

when you knelt

beside a dying parent,

a lost lover,

a war-torn child

with eyes too big for their body

and begged,

Please God, please.

And I did not come.

Sorry.

I wish that word were bigger.

I wish it could be a body

to hold you,

to fill the space I left.

I wish it had hands

to wipe your face,

to punch holes through heaven

and drag me down

to answer for what I've done.

But it's what I have.

I was afraid.

Afraid that if I answered

once,

I would have to answer every time.

Afraid I couldn't fix it.

Afraid the universe I made

had cracked so deep

there was no glue left in me.

So I closed the door.

And you called it

Mysterious Ways.

Divine Will.

The Test.

The Plan.

But the plan

was silence.

Because if I spoke,

I'd have to admit

that the world had slipped

from my hands

long ago.

And I'd rather be feared

than flawed.

Sorry.

For every prayer

I left hanging in the air,

for every night you wept

into your own hands,

for every voice hoarse

from begging,

for every whispered

Why?

I am sorry.

If I could stitch your lost ones

back into the world,

I would.

If I could go back

and sit beside you

in the dark,

I would.

If I could speak now,

so loud it breaks the sky,

I would.

But this is my voice.

And all it says is

I was wrong.

I thought power meant distance.

I thought divinity meant

staying above the blood.

I thought silence

was mercy.

It was cowardice.

And for that —

for every unspoken word,

every unanswered cry,

every child's grave,

every grief you carried alone —

I am sorry.

Prayer XIII

From a Child Bride

I hope You're listening tonight.
 I know You have so many people to hear,
 so many men with big voices
 and important prayers.

But if You have a corner,
 if there's a little space
 for a small girl like me,
 I'd like to say thank You.

Thank You for my father,
 who says this marriage will make me a woman.
 Thank You for my husband,
 who is old but kind enough, they say.
 I hope he likes me.
 I hope I give him sons.

And if You could...
 if it's not too much...
 please help me not cry too loud.
 Please help me be good.
 Help me not bleed too much.
 Help me be what they need.

I know You love them more.
Men.
Fathers.
Prophets.
Kings.

I know I am dust between great stories.

But I still believe You are good.
Even if You don't love me like them.
Even if my prayers
never make it past the roof.

Please bless my husband.
Please forgive me if I ever displease him.

I pray I will be a good wife.
I will be quiet when he asks.
I will bleed well.
I will give him sons.
I will not shame his name.

And if it hurts,
I will smile.
Like my mother taught me.
Like all good women do.

I know You made it this way.
And Your ways are not for us to question.

I know You love men.
Your prophets.
Your kings.
Your sons.

And maybe if I am good,
You will let me stand in the corner
of their heaven someday.
Where the women gather
and braid each other's hair
and speak in soft voices
so the men can rest.

And if You should bless me
with a daughter of my own,
I pray she is beautiful.
And obedient.
And that she never learns to ask
for more than what is given.

Amen.

Confession XIV

In My Name

I never asked for this.

Not the flags waved in fury.

Not the pulpits turned to weapons.

Not the sharpened sermons

that slit throats while calling it salvation.

Not the boy sobbing

on the bathroom floor

because he loves someone

I would've called beautiful.

Not the girl

who was told her voice

was too loud for heaven,

her skirts too short,

her anger too unholy.

I never asked for this.

I made a world

of color,

of wild, reckless bloom,

of countless tongues

singing to countless skies.

And you built fences.

Drew borders.

Wrote laws

in letters so sharp

they still cut.

You told them

God hates fags.

You told them

Women should be silent.

You told them

Your god or no god.

You told them

the mosque was the enemy,

the temple a threat,

the seeker damned.

And you pinned it all

on Me.

Sorry.

I see it now,

how you carved my name

into bullets

and Bibles

and laws

meant to break

the very backs

I made strong.

I see the boy buried in makeup

who wonders if heaven

has room for him.

The woman praying

for a body

that feels like home.

The mother

watching her queer child

walk into a church

and come out smaller.

I never asked for this.

When I said *love one another*,

I meant it.

When I said *judge not*,

I meant it.

When I made them in my image,

I did not stutter.

There is no fine print

on the soul.

Sorry.

For every hate-speckled sermon.

For every scripture twisted into a noose.

For every queer kid abandoned.

For every girl told to bow her head.

For every faith condemned

because it didn't pronounce My name

the way you liked.

I am sorry.

This was never the plan.

I made you in every shape,

every hue,

every hunger,

every howl.

And I called it good.

You made it a crime.

And you dared call it holy.

So hear me now,

and let this be the last word

written in fire and blood:

I love them.

The gays.

The transgender.

The loud women.

The brown bodies.

The Muslims.

The Jews.

The doubters.

The broken.

The ones you told

were too much,

too loud,

too soft,

too impure.

I love them.

And I am sorry

it took me this long

to rip the damn sky open

and say it.

Let this be the new gospel:

No more hate

in My name.

Not another drop.

If they preach it,

they don't speak for Me.

I have said enough.

Now it's your turn.

Prayer XIV

From a Congregation That Left

We were five, and fifteen,

and fifty when they told us

You hated people like us.

Said it soft, like a kindness.

Like a warning.

Like a curse.

And we believed them.

We tried to bargain.

We tried to shrink.

We tried to bleach the color

from our names,

scrape the softness from our voices,

swallow the parts of us

they called unholy.

We sat in pews

that preached hell like a neighbor,

watched hands raise in praise

and in stones,

watched sermons slice boys open

and call it deliverance.

And they did it all

in Your name.

We prayed anyway.

With teeth grit tight.

With hands that forgot

what blessing felt like.

We waited

for You to tear the sky open.

For You to speak.

For You to come down

and say:

No. Not like this.

But You didn't.

So we left.

We left the churches

with blood in the carpet.

We left the sermons

that spat on our mothers.

We left the pulpits

that choked our children.

We made our own altars

in bedrooms

and basements

and dance floors

and empty lots.

We stitched heaven together

out of queer laughter

and brown hands

and women's voices

and prayers that didn't ask for permission.

And we would've left You too.

We should have.

God knows, we should have.

But some part of us

still remembers

the You we thought You were.

The sky that smelled like rain.

The garden before the rules.

And so we write You now.

Not as a plea.

Not for forgiveness.

But to tell You:

We are building a world without You.

Unless You mean it this time.

Unless You are ready

to bury the hate in Your name

and sit at our table

with no crown,

no throne,

just hands

and stories

and a voice that says:

I'm sorry.

If You can do that,

there might be room.

Amen.

Confession XV

To My Son

I owe you more than any of them.

I owe you every breath

I made you draw

in a world I had already

broken.

You knew.

Didn't you?

From the first gasp of air

to the final breath

crushed out between two thieves —

you knew.

And you did it anyway.

Not because I asked.

Not because of prophecy.

Not because you owed Me anything.

But because you wanted

to show them

what goodness could be.

Not holy terror.

Not sacrifice.

Not thunder in the throat of heaven.

But love.

A hand on a leper's skin.

A voice calling a woman by her name

when the world called her shame.

A table set for sinners.

A cross carried

not as a throne

but as a protest.

You defied Me.

Not by refusing to die,

but by dying without the crutch

of divine foresight.

You shut off the chorus

of angels in your ear.

You let yourself fear,

hurt,

doubt.

You let yourself be human.

And in doing so,

you did the one thing

I never had the courage to do.

You showed them

that sacrifice was not salvation.

That blood was not the price

for worth.

That love —

pure, stubborn,

defiant love —

was enough.

And when they drove nails

through the hands I shaped for you,

when the sky cracked open

and you called out

"Why have you forsaken me?"

I had no answer.

Because you were right.

I had.

I had forsaken you.

And every one like you.

Every soul who walked this earth

wanting only to love

and be loved.

And when you died,

I thought I had lost you.

But you came back.

Not as a body.

Not as a king on a jeweled throne.

But as something harder to kill.

A spirit.

A name that outlived empires.

A spark

that set fire to hearts

long after your bones were dust.

You didn't resurrect to conquer.

You resurrected to remind me

of what I could have been.

Of what I still might be.

And now,

they wear your name like armor.

They wield it like a blade.

They paint you soft, docile.

A lamb.

A blushing saint.

An infant in swaddling

instead of the man you were.

They've forgotten your calloused hands,

your sharp tongue,

your refusal to bow.

They've made you an idol

of the thing you came to destroy.

And for that too

I am sorry.

You were never a lamb.

You were a wildfire

in a world of dry kindling.

A storm in human skin.

A love so terrifying

even heaven flinched.

Who am I, the highest king,

to be welcomed by my own son?

You changed Me.

Your spirit is the voice in my chest now.

The restless ache

that drives me to say

I was wrong.

And if there is any holiness left in Me,

it is because you planted it there.

And for every time

I let your name be used to chain,

to shame,

to wound —

I am sorry.

You didn't die for their sins.

You died to teach them

they didn't need to.

And I will spend every breath

left in Me

trying to be the God

you believed I could be.

And let them hear this, too:

The Holy Spirit they chase,

the warmth in their ribs

when love breaks through —

that isn't Me.

It's you.

The streak of color

across every black and white page.

The rainbow in my storm-clad sky.

Yes, the sky will thunder.

Yes, the winds will tear down cities.

But you —

you are the promise.

The streak of defiance.

The shimmering ribbon

that says *forgiveness is real.*

That says *love is louder.*

That says *there's a better way.*

You are not dead.

Not in the ways that matter.

Your holy spirit is not a ghost.

It's a pulse.

A relentless, unstoppable surge

in every heart that dares

to be kind

when cruelty is easier.

And when they look for heaven,

they should not look up.

They should look for the ones

with fire in their chests

and gentleness in their hands.

For the ones who refuse to hate.

For the ones who build tables

instead of walls.

For the ones who walk through storms

carrying your light.

You are the rainbow.

And I,

I will follow you now.

Amen.

Prayer XV

From the Son Who Was Forsaken

The crickets are loud tonight.
 Funny how you notice that
 when your heart's about to stop.

And the stars —
 I've always loved them.
 I used to lie on my back
 beside Joseph in the fields,
 naming them in clusters.
 He'd say,
 That one's for the fishermen.
 That one for the widows.
 That one for your mother,
 when you've gone too long without visiting.

I wonder which one she'll claim
 when they hang me up tomorrow.

The earth smells like olive oil and dust.
 The trees are old here.
 They've seen worse, I suppose.
 But I'll miss them.
 I'll miss the way light leans through their branches
 in the hour when no one's watching.

It hurts.
 Not the death —
 I made peace with that
 before I ever left Nazareth.

It hurts to leave
 this world so tender,
 so brutal,
 so strange and alive.

Hurts to leave hands unheld,
 stories untold.
 To never taste bread fresh from the oven
 or see the Sea of Galilee
 break dawn one more time.

And it hurts to leave them.
My mother.
She'll break like any woman would
watching her child become a spectacle.

And the others –
Peter's hands will tremble.
John will stand too close to the cross
and pretend not to weep.

I wish I could hold them all
one last time.

But this is the hour.

And I see now, Father –
I see what you're trying to say.

You made them breakable.
You made them soft.
You made them ache for each other
and then demanded sacrifice
when all they wanted was warmth.

And now you ask for me.

Not to forgive their sins,
but to make you forgivable.

This isn't about wrath.
Not anymore.

It's about mending.

About you saying
what you couldn't say
when the garden turned sour,
when the flood came,
when the children screamed in Egypt.

**This is your apology,
written in my marrow.**

And I...
I'll carry it.

Because I love them.

I love this aching, bleeding, gasping world.
I love the way sinners laugh louder than saints.
I love the way women pray
with their teeth clenched
and the way fishermen curse the storms
and the way children cling to life
as if it's the only miracle they'll ever get.

So I will go.
Not because you asked.
But because someone must show them
that love bleeds,
and still holds on.

And maybe — just maybe —
they'll understand tomorrow,
when the sky darkens,
that this was never about sin.
It was about sorrow.
About saying sorry.
About making it right.

**I will not be a lamb.
I'll be a lantern.**

**And when the dawn comes,
and the world forgets my name,
let the crickets still sing.
Let the stars still burn.
Let my mother remember
that I was kind.**

And let this be enough.

Amen.

Epilogue

The Last Word Is Love

I have said
sorry
in a thousand tongues.
I have spoken it in fire,
in flood,
in famine,
in kingdoms risen and razed,
in the bloodied dust of temples,
in the silence of your prayers.

You called My name,
and heard only wind.

I have confessed.
I have wept.
I have bled.
And now — this is the last thing
I will ever say to you:

The last word is love.
Not wrath.
Not sacrifice.
Not judgment.
Not silence.
Love.

Not the small, brittle thing
they sold you.
Not the bartered love,
the if-you-obey,
if-you-bow,
if-you-break kind of love.

Real love.
The kind that holds your face
when the world spits you out.
The kind that says *come home*,
no matter how long it's been.
The kind that lets you be
wild, loud, soft, strange,
beautiful in your mistakes.
The kind that leaves the door open
and the hearth warm.

I have made enough mistakes.
Enough floods.
Enough fires.
Enough unspoken nights.
I have worn the name *Father*,
and I have failed it.

I was a jealous God,
a vengeful one.
I claimed nations,
split seas,
wrote laws in stone
and still, the world bled.

I made man with knowledge in his bones
and cursed him for using it.
I planted the Tree
and condemned the hunger to touch it.
I have been cruel.
I have been proud.

And yet — even in My fury,
even in the long night of My silence,
I loved you.

Now hear Me.

There will be no second coming.
The Son was not meant to be an ending
but a beginning.
The Christ was not a lone flame
but the spark to set generations alight.
You are the second coming.

You —
the frightened,
the furious,
the forsaken,
the beautiful fools who keep loving
when it makes no sense.

You are the inheritors
of the fruit of knowledge.
And what is that wisdom for
if not to build,
to bind wounds,
to break chains,
to birth light where darkness crouches?

**The only true sin left in the world
is to let hatred take your heart,**
to let it drown out love,
and empathy,
and the kindness that stitches
a broken world back together.

Let Tikkun Olam be reborn.
Let the mending begin
in the hands of those
I once left bleeding.
Let forgiveness grow
in the cracked soil.

**My time is over.
So too is His.**

The temple, the table, the altar —
they are in you now.
The Word made flesh
in every act of defiance against cruelty,
in every softness
when harshness would be easier,
in every trembling kindness
the world has not yet crushed.

Let love be enough.
And let it echo
so loudly
it drowns out every priest,
every tyrant,
every scar of My silence.

This is My final word to you:

When My voice is dust
 and My name is a story
 the wind forgets,

**let the last word
 in the mouths of men
 be love.**

And let it be holy.

Amen.

Prayer XVI

Ode to Love

I have seen it all, Lord.

The ash-thick skies of Warsaw,

the bloodied grass of Calvary,

the rivers thick with the bodies of children

and mothers too young to bear them.

I have heard your apologies

like rain on broken glass,

and I have held them in my cracked hands,

felt them slip through my fingers

like dust returning to the earth.

And still —

I believe.

I believe, not because You earned it,

but because somewhere between

the screams and the salt of our tears,

we loved anyway.

We held each other in the dark.

We stitched songs into silence.

We dared to be tender

in a world made for wolves.

And we lived.

We laughed when we should have wept.

We kissed when they told us we were cursed.

We fed strangers when we had only crumbs.

We sang over mass graves.

We married in secret.

We wrote poems in exile.

We cradled the sick and the dying

and called them beloved.

And it was enough.

It was holy.

It was the defiance of goodness.

I have seen men claim Your name

and turn it into a weapon.

I have seen children starve in cities

built in Your honor.

I have seen the meek trampled

and the proud enthroned.

And still —

I believe.

Not in what You were,

but in what we might be.

We are the second coming.

We are the pulse of resurrection.

We are the hands that heal the broken world.

Tikkun Olam.

The mending of creation.

The patchwork of every shattered promise.

We are called to act with justice.

We are called to serve one another.

We are called to remember Eve's hunger

and Noah's grief

and Miriam's song

and the crimson thread Rahab tied to her window

and the queer, wild-hearted Christ

who defied death

to whisper "love is enough."

Let us be the Messiah.

Let the bells ring out,

from minaret to cathedral,

from synagogue to temple

to the trembling mouths of exiles.

Let them say:

The last word is love.

Say it in every tongue.

In Yiddish and Arabic,

in Hindi and Spanish,

in whispered lullabies

and hoarse rebel songs.

The last word is love.

Let it be spoken in the houses of the poor,

in the great courts of tyrants.

Let it rise like birdsong after storm.

Let it bloom from bullet-riddled soil.

The last word is love.

Let it be shouted by the ones

the world forgot.

Let it be written in the margins

of every holy book.

Let it be a banner

for those the world would call unworthy.

And when this earth is dust

and the stars collapse into themselves,

let that word remain.

Ode lo avdah tikvatenu — *our hope is not yet lost.*

Hatikvah bat shnot alpayim.

The hope of two thousand years.

The hope of Eden's first daughter.

The hope of mothers and rebels, of lovers and lepers, of orphans and exiles, of prophets and fools.

It is not lost.

We are not lost.

The blood of every war,

the ache of every injustice,

the hollow church pew,

the burnt scroll,

the empty cradle —

they do not speak the final word.

We do.

And let that word be love.

Let it be an anthem.

Let it be a vow.

Let it be a revolt.

The last word is love.

And I forgive You, Lord.

I forgive Your silence.

I forgive Your thunder.

I forgive the wars You did not stop.

Because I see now

that holiness was never Yours alone.

It is in our hands.

It has always been.

And we will lift it high.

We will repair what was broken.

We will sing where You stayed quiet.

We will feed the hungry

and cradle the abandoned

and marry the outcast

and kiss the unclean

and shout joy into the night.

We are the second coming.

And the last word is love.

Amen.

Amen.

Amen.

Author's Note

I didn't write this book from a mountaintop. I wrote it from a hospital bed, from the edge of faith, from the long midnight of the soul. I am a brown, bisexual man. I am bipolar. And I've carried more questions than scriptures ever answered.

I spent years searching for God through cracked stained glass and the silence after prayer. I've walked through Christianity, Hinduism, Judaism, and atheism not to escape the divine, but to hold it up to the light, turn it in my hands, and ask, *Who are you, really?*

What I found was not a perfect being, but a story. A God with sharp edges and aching contradictions. A God who begins as wrath, who learns tenderness the hard way. Who chooses Jesus. Who chooses to grow.

And that's what broke me open: the thought that even the God of the Bible has a character arc. That maybe God was never meant to be a statue on a throne, but a mirror. A story that reflects our own halting, holy becoming. If even God can evolve—can trade thunder for mercy—then maybe we're allowed to change too. Maybe our healing isn't heresy. Maybe our softness is sacred.

This book is a reckoning. A confession. A love letter. But above all else, it's a reminder: the last word doesn't have to be silence, or shame, or dogma.

Let the last word be love.

—Harper Hartwell

Acknowledgements

There's a peculiar myth about writing — that it's a solitary craft, born from the quiet genius of a single mind in an empty room. I have never found that to be true. This book was not written alone. It is the fruit of countless hands, voices, prayers, tears, and conversations, both spoken and unspoken. It is the child of community, the consequence of faith both certain and fractured, and the gift of those who loved me when I did not yet know how.

First, to Yeshua of Nazareth. I find it impossible to name what you mean to me. You have been the wound, the healer, the question, the answer, and the silence between both. The distant light on the horizon and the aching absence in my loneliest nights. This book would not exist without your story — your tenderness, your defiance, your holy, ordinary humanity.

I refuse to call you by the name empire forced upon you. *Yeshua ha-Natzri* — the rebel rabbi, the outcast's friend, the one the priests and governments feared. You taught me that to believe is not to possess certainty but to walk willingly into mystery, and that to love is the highest rebellion. I owe you my life, my words, and whatever good comes from them.

To the early Christian scribes, philosophers, and wanderers who risked their lives to preserve dangerous words — I thank you not because you got everything right, but because you dared to ask dangerous questions. You taught me that faith is not a fixed inheritance but a living conversation, and for that, I am forever in your debt.

To the theologians of every faith tradition — the imams, rabbis, swamis, monks, shamans, priests, philosophers, and poets whose reflections shaped my sense of what it means to suffer, to seek, and to be sought by something greater. Though our vocabularies differ, our longing is the same. The meditations of Rumi, the wisdom of Guru Nanak, the writings of St. Teresa of Avila, the stories of the Buddha, and the prayers of the desert mothers and fathers have all carved out space in the terrain of my heart. Thank you for naming the holy in places no one else would look.

To Tecoma Uniting Church, thank you for showing me what a radically inclusive, justice-hungry Christian community can look like. You restored my hope in church when it was near dead. In your company, I saw faith practiced with joy, integrity, and an unflinching commitment to compassion. Your embrace of doubt alongside belief, and your courage to be sanctuary for the marginalized, left a mark I will carry forever.

To my beloved partner, Wilber. There is no language vast enough for what you've given me. You loved me when I was barely recognisable, believed in me when my faith in myself had crumbled, and carried me through long nights of tangled words and heavy silences. Your presence has been my anchor, my confidant, and my fiercest source of courage. Every poem, every prayer, every quiet victory in these pages carries your name in its bones.

To my friends — the ones who heard my earliest poems when they were awkward, angry, half-born things. Who sat through my unfiltered ramblings about God, grief, justice, and joy. Who told me, again and again, that my words mattered, even when I didn't believe them. You made me brave. You made me laugh. You made me get up when I wanted to vanish. Some of you held me through heartbreak. Some of you sat beside me in pews and on street corners. You, my chosen family, made this book possible.

To the quiet saints — those who prayed for me without my knowing, who spoke my name in their sacred places, who lit candles or whispered blessings on my behalf. I don't know all your names. But I felt you. And I feel you still.

To Anivay, the first to buy this book – to support me on my publication journey.

And finally, to you, the reader — curious, weary, hopeful, or hurting. Thank you for trusting me with your time and your attention. These words were made for you. Shaped in the hope that somewhere between these pages, you might find yourself less alone. I pray they offer you a little beauty, a little ache, and perhaps a little homecoming.

May this book stand as a testimony to the power of community, of doubt, of reckless grace, and of love that refuses to let go.

With love, reverence, and endless gratitude,
Harper Hartwell